# DINOFOURS™

## I'M NOT YOUR FRIEND!

For Nancy – S.M.

Scholastic Children's Books,
Commonwealth House, 1-19 New Oxford Street,
London WC1A 1NU, UK
a division of Scholastic Ltd

London ~ New York ~ Toronto ~ Sydney ~ Auckland

First published in the US by Scholastic Inc., 1996
This edition published in the UK by Scholastic Ltd, 1997

Text copyright © Scholastic Inc., 1996
Illustrations © Hans Wilhelm Inc., 1996

ISBN 0 590 19832 7

Printed in Italy by Amadeus S.p.A.

# DINOFOURS™

## I'M NOT YOUR FRIEND!

by Steve Metzger
Illustrated by Hans Wilhelm

Hippo

Tracy and Danielle were best friends.
They did almost everything together at school.

During indoor playtime, they painted rainbows at the same easel. Tracy always made a red arc on the bottom. Danielle always painted a blue arc on the top.

When they went outside, they played cats and dogs.
Tracy liked being the mischievous kitten who tried to
run away from home. Danielle was the puppy who
made sure she didn't.

And they always sat next to each other at circle time.
And snack time. And at lunchtime, too. The other
children could sit on either side of Danielle and Tracy,
but no one – absolutely no one – could sit between them.

When their teacher, Mrs Dee, wanted to find Tracy, she only had to find Danielle. Tracy was sure to be near by. And whenever she wanted to find Danielle, spotting Tracy was all she needed to do.

Then one day, Danielle saw Albert making clay bunnies. She thought this might be fun. So Danielle joined Albert at the clay table. Meanwhile, Tracy was gluing wood scraps at the art table. She spotted Danielle across the room.

"Danielle!" shouted Tracy. "I'm making a tall tower. It's fun. Come here and help me."

"Not now, Tracy," said Danielle. "I'm making clay bunnies with Albert. I'll play with you later!"

Tracy did not like what Danielle had just said to her.
Not one bit! Danielle was her friend. And nobody else's! She
stomped over to the clay table and pulled on Danielle's arm.

"You're not Albert's friend," she yelled. "You're my friend!
You have to play with me."

"Stop it!" shouted Danielle as she freed herself from Tracy's
grasp. "I want to play with Albert now. Leave me alone."

"I'm really cross with you!" Tracy shouted as she walked away and sat down in a corner.
If Danielle plays with Albert, she can't be my friend, Tracy thought. Now I don't have any friends. I want to go home. Tracy made up a song about how she felt.

"I have no friends.
I'm all alone.
Danielle is bad,
And I'm so sad!"

She sang this song over and over to herself.

Mrs Dee noticed Tracy sitting in the cloakroom.

"What's wrong, Tracy?" she asked.

"Danielle is playing with Albert," Tracy said. "She doesn't like me any more. She's not my friend!"

"Oh, Tracy," said Mrs Dee. "Even though Danielle is playing with Albert, she's still your friend, too. Perhaps you'd like to play with someone else."

"I don't want to play with anyone else," Tracy said. "I just want to be here by myself."

"Well, okay," said Mrs Dee as she walked away. "But if you change your mind, I'm sure there are lots of children who would love to play with you."

"Never!" said Tracy. "Danielle was my only friend." Then, Tracy sang her song.

"I have no friends.
I'm all alone.
Danielle is bad,
And I'm so sad!"

While Tracy sang her song, she heard one of the children calling out.
"All aboard! All aboard the Special Train!"
It was Joshua, wearing a train driver's cap.

What is that silly Joshua shouting about? Tracy wondered. What's a Special Train? Then she heard him again.

"All aboard! All aboard the Special Train!" Tracy walked slowly over to the row of chairs that Joshua was using for his train.

"Joshua, what's so special about this train?" Tracy asked.

"It's a flying train," said Joshua. "First, it's going to America. Then to Africa and the North Pole. Last stop – the moon!"

"Wow!" said Tracy. "This is a special train. I want to buy a ticket."

"There are no tickets," said Joshua. "I'm the only person in this game and I'm the driver."

"I can be the ticket seller," said Tracy. "I'll cut out tickets from paper and sell them over there."

"That's a great idea," said Joshua. Tracy found some paper and a pair of scissors. She quickly cut out lots of tickets. She even made a "Ticket Seller's" hat. When Tracy finished, Mrs Dee helped her write a "Tickets" sign. Tracy wrote the first letter. That was easy. "T" was the first letter in her name. Now Tracy was ready.

"Tickets!" Tracy shouted. "Tickets for the Special Train! It's going to America, Africa, the North Pole and the moon. Get your tickets here!"

The other children lined up to buy tickets. Even Mrs Dee joined the line. Tracy and Joshua were happy to see so many people riding on the Special Train. When a lot of tickets had been sold, Tracy became the conductor and collected them.

Tracy and Joshua took turns being the driver.
"This is fun!" Tracy said to Joshua.
"Let's play this game tomorrow, too."
"All right," said Joshua.

Just then, Danielle walked over.
"Hello, Tracy," said Danielle.
"Can I buy a ticket for the Special Train?"

When Tracy saw Danielle, her smile quickly became a frown.

"No!" said Tracy. "There are no more tickets. You can't come on the Special Train." Danielle looked as if she might cry.
Mrs Dee leaned over.

"I can see a seat behind me," she said. "I think you might have one more ticket."

"Oh, all right," said Tracy. "You can come on the Special Train. But don't make a mess!"

"I won't," said Danielle as she sat down.

Later on, Tracy was the driver again. Danielle moved to the seat behind her.

"Tracy," Danielle said. "It was fun playing with Albert, but you're still my best friend."

"I am?" said Tracy. "I thought you didn't want to play with me any more."

"Of course, I do!" said Danielle. "I can play with Albert and still play with you, too."

"That means I can play with Joshua," said Tracy, "and still be your best friend."

"That's right!" said Danielle.

Tracy said, "This really is a Special Train – because we're on it together!"

Then Tracy sang a new song.

"Danielle is my friend.
My very best friend.
I was cross and sad.
But now I'm really glad."